A Bride For David

By

Elizabeth Castle

Chapter One

"And I think David will be perfect."

David Bennett heard his name spoken in a soft British accent and scowled at the woman at the front of the room. "David is perfect for what?"

Juliet Torrance, who had gotten used to David ignoring pretty much everything going on around him during any type of meeting, ignored him in turn. "The campaign is all about transparency. Showing the lab and how things are made will be a great way to show not only consumers but potential clients what they are getting when they buy products from Brown Chemical Labs. They're getting products made by a family, a family just like theirs, and one that cares about what goes in and on their bodies."

David scowled at Juliet. The woman got on his nerves. She'd been with the company two months, but it seemed much longer. His cousin Evelyn and her husband Sebastian had convinced everyone she was just what the company needed. Sebastian had worked with Juliet when he'd lived overseas and said she was the best. The board agreed that bringing in someone from the outside to help revitalize the company's image was the best plan.

At the time, David had simply agreed so he could get back to his lab. He might hold a fifth of the family company's shares, and he might be on the board, but as far as he was concerned, whatever his family did with the company was fine by him, so long as he had full control of the lab and the work he did. Once upon a time, he'd had to care, but with Sebastian firmly in control, he'd gratefully stepped down from active management to focus on what he cared about. His lab.

But now that Juliet Torrance was here, he was anything but pleased with the decision. She was forever poking around his lab, asking all sorts of questions. She had a tablet and stylus that she carried with her everywhere she went and took notes constantly. But when she invaded his space, he told her in no uncertain terms where she could go with her precious tablet and her incessant questions.

What ticked him off was that she pretty much ignored him while he raged at her. Her pretty blue eyes always held a sparkle of mischief, her wavy blond hair always framed her perfectly oval face, and her lush lips were always shaped into a hint of a smile, as if she was secretly laughing at him. She was classically beautiful, but all he saw when he looked at her was a pain in his backside. As of yet, he had not found a way to stop her or discourage her. She would nod, make some kind of remark in that soft voice of hers, and then go about what she came to do. She was a steamroller in a tiny blond package. She was barely over five feet, but she was quite a force to be reckoned with.

David shifted uncomfortably in his seat. "I said, David is perfect for what?"

Juliet simply raised an eyebrow at him.

Evelyn piped in. "You're the driving force behind our brand. The products you work on and create every day are what keep Brown alive. The past year and a half has been rough. Clients and customers are not sure they should trust us. We want to show them who we are and what we do. To that effect, Juliet has constructed several campaigns to show them those things through print and video marketing. Sebastian and I will work on the financial side. You will work on the production side."

David looked over the slide on the projection screen. It seemed Juliet had not only taken notes with her tablet but pictures as well. Mockups of him in the lab, along with an ad campaign message, finally got his attention.

"No way." David rose from his seat.

Sebastian stood from his seat at the head of the table. "I think this is exactly what we need. Andrew has been quite vocal in the press, despite the fact he's behind bars. He's taken it upon himself to start a smear campaign. As much as

I hate to admit it, he has been somewhat successful. He's been playing the martyr from his wheelchair, acting like he's an innocent victim. Certain members of the press have been spinning the story to make it look like we manipulated the situation and that we're at fault for what happened to him. And when people know someone was able to successfully embezzle money from you, their faith in your business practices waver. We need you to help undo that."

David scowled at his cousin-in-law. "How exactly am I supposed to do that?"

Juliet took back command of the meeting and waved at her presentation. "You're going to be the new face for the brand. We'll clean you up a bit, get you a new lab coat that doesn't have ten years of stains on it, and show the world how much Brown cares about what is in our products. You'll walk them through the lab, the processes, and the outcomes. You'll show them we are fully committed to quality control in our labs and only deliver the safest products to the market."

David was starting to panic. "You want me to do what?"

Juliet let out an exasperated sigh. "Get used to the idea. You can't wiggle out of this one. You're an attractive, mature male, and with the right spin, we can play you off as one who's caring and compassionate while being dedicated to his work and the products you create. Women buy a lot of products, and they'll trust a middle-aged man with a killer smile."

David's voice got rough. "Middle-aged?"

Sebastian stopped the tirade he knew was coming. "Sorry, David, but you're our man. The other option would be to hire another chemist, one who wants to play this part. But something tells me you'd hate that idea even more. And we can't just hire an actor. People would find out and be furious with us for deceiving them."

David turned his attention back to Sebastian. "Why not put you, Evelyn, and your baby in the campaign? Heck, you could get Kimberly and John and their two kids, and Leslie and Philip and their kid. Just slap a bunch of cute babies and toddlers in the ads and you'll have those same women wrapped around your fingers."

Juliet turned her presentation off and picked up her tablet. "You're missing the point, David. But that doesn't surprise me since you haven't paid attention to a word I've said in the past hour. You and I will meet first thing Monday and start going over the script and what I need you to bring for the videos. We'll start with the photos. I have a stylist who can make anyone look good. We'll have to tackle that mess you call hair and get you a decent shave, but otherwise, I think just a little makeup and some new clothes will do the trick."

David ran a hand through his hair. Okay, so yeah, he needed a haircut. And yes, he probably could stand to shave. But listening to Little Miss Britain dismiss him so thoroughly rankled. "Sorry, I'm growing a beard. It could be a good look for the campaign."

Evelyn's and Sebastian's snickers were heard clearly in the quiet room. David ignored them. Juliet was glaring at him; for once, her eyes were shooting fire and her lips were

pursed. Good. He got up and left

Chapter Two

It had taken the weekend for Juliet to cool down. David Bennett had the distinction of being one of the few people who managed to get under her skin. Juliet liked to think she was a calm sort, always ready and able to tackle any problem. Being in marketing could be a rough job, especially when one specialized in public relations and fixing tarnished reputations as she did. She was the one businesses called when they needed to turn their image around or get themselves out of the fire of some business or social media disaster.

When Sebastian had called her and asked her if she would be interested in taking a position with his company, she hadn't had to think about it long. She didn't have family, so leaving London hadn't been an issue. She supposed she had friends, but most of them were more business acquaintances. And her last relationship had died a quick but painful death more than a year earlier. Sebastian had told her he needed her unique skill set, and coming to America seemed like the change she had been seeking in her life. She'd immediately started filing the necessary paperwork to take the job in California.

She knew the story of how the company had gotten into this position in the first place. Sebastian had inherited a fifth of the company he had worked for before he had moved to London. He was one of five owners, and the only one not family. In short order, he found himself involved with Evelyn Bennett, previous president of Brown. Ultimately it had been Evelyn's secretary who had been embezzling funds and trying to exact revenge on Evelyn's ex-fiancé, Andrew Shepherd. Andrew had also embezzled from the company a few years before that, and the secretary had been in on it. She had attempted to kill Evelyn, but Evelyn had thought it was Andrew. Andrew had embezzled and started his relationship with Evelyn in a misguided plan for revenge against Evelyn's mother, with whom he'd had a tumultuous affair.

The story had seemed complicated to Juliet, one she had heard in pieces over the past two months. In the end, the secretary was in jail, and Andrew was spinning lies from his wheelchair behind bars, a wheelchair the secretary was responsible for putting him in. When Andrew had started talking to the press, Sebastian had not been worried about it much. He and Evelyn had just welcomed their first child, and their focus had been on the new baby. But little Bridgette was now nine months old, and Sebastian had started noticing drops in their sales and clients who were pulling back. So he'd called her to help fix it.

So now she had to deal with David. David with his chocolate brown hair and eyes. He was on the leaner side, but his shoulders filled out a jacket, and his chest was broad enough to catch a girl's eye. He was under six feet, though not by much, but with her smaller stature, he loomed over her. He was handsome, but what drew her was how smart he was. Evelyn and Sebastian might run the company, but David was the one who created the products the company sold, and in her mind, he was the heart and soul of the company. It was too bad he could be such a jerk.

But it was David she had to deal with if she was going to be successful in her campaign to rebuild Brown's reputation. First and foremost, she wanted Evelyn, Sebastian, and David to rename the company. Evelyn wasn't sure, Sebastian thought the idea might have merit, and David was vehemently opposed. His grandfather had started Brown, and Brown it would remain. She was pretty sure she would never get David to agree, but she had hopes she could convince Evelyn and Sebastian to outvote him over time. Brown Chemicals sounded like a company that made paint thinner or bug spray. It didn't sound like a family company that made a combination of everyday products for the home and beauty products that were good for the environment and the health and wellness of those using the beauty line.

So here she was, standing in her underwear on a Monday morning, staring at her clothes, trying to find just the right outfit for her confrontation with David. She knew he would be against being photographed and recorded, but his face was the one she wanted. Sebastian was a well-known figure in the community, and he was part of her campaign strategy. Sebastian was the financial face of the company, the one who would defend and help define Brown's vision and future. And yes, Evelyn would be by his side, and if Juliet could work in the baby, she knew it wouldn't hurt to show the perfect family to the community. But David was the face behind the product, and that was what she needed from him.

Juliet finally settled on a pale yellow suit and a white blouse. The fitted jacket cinched her waist, and the skirt fell to just above her knees. It suited her pale coloring and made her think of spring flowers. She wore a small pair of diamonds in her ears and a small garnet, her birthstone, on her right hand. It had been a gift from her mother on her sixteenth birthday.

She took care with her makeup, keeping the colors soft, and colored her lips with a pale pink shade. She also took extra care with her hair, taking a little extra time to get the natural wave just right. Satisfied that she looked her best and most professional, she grabbed her purse and tablet and headed to the office for what she was sure would be an unpleasant morning.

She first stopped in her office and checked her morning emails. She answered what was pressing, then she grabbed her tablet and headed to the lab. She greeted everyone on her way there, smiling and chatting as she went. The company was relatively small, so she was getting to know everyone by name.

She pushed through the double doors that led to the lab where a handful of people were already hard at work. David had his back to her, his nose buried in a stack of papers. It was well known throughout the building that David hated computers and was apt to be found working off printed paper rather than his screen. She came up behind him and noticed how close his nose was to the printout.

"Where are your glasses?"

David's head shot up at Juliet's voice. "I suppose it was too much to hope you wouldn't show up."

Juliet glanced around and grabbed his glasses off his very messy desk and handed them to him. "I was hoping you would have thought it over while at home this weekend and come to the intelligent conclusion. If you think about it hard enough, you'll know I'm right."

Sometimes he wasn't sure if she was pointing out what she thought was right or if she was insulting his intelligence. The worst part was she usually was right. This weekend was no exception. He had thought it over, and as much as it pained him, he understood her logic. Sebastian was also right. He did not want someone else in his lab messing with his formulas. He had staff under him, but everything they did came through him.

David figured he might as well concede now. "What do we do first?"

Juliet gave him a brilliant smile and flipped open the cover on her tablet. "The first thing you need to do is clear your schedule for your appointment with my stylist. I have some options here that I think would best suit you."

David scowled. He took the tablet from her. He had a

barber he saw regularly, not a stylist. And these styles were not to his liking. "What am I doing, auditioning for the cover of GQ?"

Juliet pointed to the first style. "I'm partial to this one. I thought since you are becoming attached to your beard, or what currently passes for one, this style would suit it best. We could just let a little more facial hair grow and have it styled. You'll look great."

David scratched the hair on his chin. He didn't normally sport a beard, but when he was in the middle of a project, he was apt to forgo some of his normal routines, and shaving usually was the first thing to go. But he was growing rather attached to it.

Juliet's eyes went serious. "Look, you don't have to keep it forever. As soon as the campaign is done, you can cut it all off again. I have twelve years of experience in marketing and public relations. Trust me, this is the way to go. You'll be one handsome bloke when I'm done. Your girlfriend will probably appreciate it, too."

"Or help me land a new one. I'm in between right now."

Juliet kept her head down and pulled up the campaign schedule. David was a serial dater, or so she'd been told. She'd only seen him with one woman since she'd met him, but if she was an indicator of the type of woman he dated, it was no wonder. She had not been too bright, and her laugh was annoying. She didn't know how he could spend more than short periods of time with her.

But Juliet figured none of that was any of her business. "Trust me, then. We'll get you all fixed up and you'll have women falling at your feet. Wednesday was the earliest I could get you an appointment for your hair. We'll see what the beard looks like in a couple of days and go from there. Thursday we can get the photographer in to take some test shots. Find the best way to light you and the room. And you might want to take a moment to clean off your desk. Then by Monday next week, we should be ready to start shooting."

David leaned back against the counter. "There's just one problem with that, sweetheart. Thursday is Thanksgiving, and we've closed the office on Friday."

Juliet frowned and looked at her calendar. "I must have

forgotten to mark that off. Do you think we could get people to work on the holiday?"

David gaped. "Uh, no, I don't think you're going to get people to work on Thursday. People will be eating until they burst and watching football or going shopping. You're not going to find anyone willing to give up their plans for a photo shoot. As for me, I'll be at the family home with a turkey drumstick in my mouth and a football game on the big screen."

Juliet sighed and marked her calendar off. "Now that would not be the right look with you shoveling food down your gullet. I'll have to schedule the test shoot for next Monday then. Just be sure you don't miss the appointment with the stylist. I had to beg to get you in. Told them it was an emergency."

"Seriously, an emergency? It's a haircut, Juliet, not surgery."

Juliet knew she tended to be a little dramatic, but in this case, it was an emergency. She needed these campaigns out last month. The campaign should have been well underway before the holidays. She knew they would only be able to get one out before Christmas.

Juliet snapped her tablet case shut. "Since I have no choice, I'll be back on Monday. But do take the opportunity to clean up around here. Otherwise, I'll have the cleaning crew come in and declutter it for you."

Chapter Three

Juliet still wasn't sure what she was doing outside Sebastian and Evelyn's home with what the lady at the bakery assured her was a traditional pecan pie in her hands. Yesterday before everyone left to enjoy the holiday, Sebastian realized Juliet had nowhere to go. She had argued she wasn't American, so while she could appreciate the sentiment of Thanksgiving, she would be perfectly fine back at her flat tweaking her campaign. Sebastian had argued with her until he wore her down, and she promised to join his family for the holiday.

Juliet tucked her wallet back in her pocket after paying the taxi driver, balancing the pie in her free hand. She hadn't decided yet if it would be worth getting a car. She hadn't had one back in London and figured she didn't need one here. Her flat was near work, so it seemed unnecessary.

But Sebastian and Evelyn's home was on the outskirts of town. Juliet wasn't sure if this was considered the country or not, but back in England, she would have deemed it such. The house was stately and would have done the English countryside proud. From what she could tell from just the outdoor lighting, the gingerbread trim was white, and the house was a light blue. The flower boxes were still blooming with bright flowers. Being in California in November was a sight different from London.

The barn off to the side was painted similar colors. She could see fencing and knew Evelyn kept a horse. Juliet supposed one day Brittany would get her very own pony and learn to ride like her mother. It was a nice feeling knowing some family traditions lived on.

She walked the short path to the porch, and before she reached the door, it opened.

Sebastian waved her in. "I saw lights pull up, then saw

them leave."

"My taxi." Juliet stepped over the threshold. The wooden floors gleamed under the entryway chandelier. The house immediately opened up into a cozy sitting area.

"I forgot you don't have a car. I should have made David stop to pick you up. You don't live far from him."

Juliet made a noncommittal sound and handed Sebastian the pie. "I wasn't sure what to bring."

"It's not a mince pie, but it will do."

Juliet gave Sebastian a small smile. He had never been fond of British food, but he had liked the mince pie she'd made one Christmas when they'd worked together.

Evelyn came in carrying Brittany. "We're so glad you could come."

Juliet held her arms out to Brittany, who accepted her invitation. She held the child to her chest while Brittany immediately started playing with her necklace. "Thank you for the invitation. I had forgotten it was a holiday until David reminded me."

Sebastian led the way toward the kitchen. "Everyone is here already. David is in the back watching football with John and Philip. I think Kimberly might be back there, too. Her son Patrick is a budding fan. Anne and Leslie are in the kitchen finishing up."

Juliet knew John from the office since he was Sebastian's executive assistant. She had not met Philip but knew he was married to David's sister, Leslie, whom she had also not met. She believed Leslie and Philip's son was named Peter. She'd met Kimberly, Patrick, and the youngest child, Josephine. Anne was a widow and the matriarch of the family.

As they neared the back of the house and went past the kitchen, the noise level increased. The children were playing on the carpet in front of the television. John and another man she assumed was Philip were cheering. Kimberly sat next to John on the floor, playing with the children.

Sebastian introduced Juliet to those she didn't know and left her with the group.

A brunette popped in behind her. "Hi, I'm Leslie. I just

wanted to say hi."

"Nice to meet you." Juliet shook the woman's hand. She was lovely, with a similar look to her brother, with the same chocolate hair and eyes.

Juliet turned back to the group when Leslie immediately went back to the kitchen. She set Brittany down to play when she began to wriggle. When she turned, she saw the only open seat was next to David. She started to cross the room, then stopped. His hair was cropped much shorter than before in the style she'd picked out. The beard had been trimmed down and was now a more discreet goatee and mustache.

"What?" David saw Juliet staring at him.

"You did what I asked."

David ran a hand through his hair. He still wasn't sure about it. He had to admit he looked good, but this was not how he was used to seeing himself. "Yeah, well, I said I'd cooperate."

Juliet gave him a small, satisfied smile and took a seat next to him. He was leaning back on the couch, quiet as he watched the game. It somehow didn't surprise her that his concentration went beyond his lab. Unlike most others in the room, he watched the game intently and didn't cheer or boo the players.

Juliet watched for a little while but was completely lost. She nudged David. "What is the point of this?"

David scowled. "The point of what?"

"American football."

David had no interest in explaining the nuances of the game to her. "The point is to get that ball to the end of the field and score."

John handed Juliet a bowl of caramel, butter, and cheese popcorn and began explaining the finer points of the game. Within twenty minutes or so, she thought she might have gotten the idea. Thankfully dinner was being served, and she didn't have to spend any more time sitting next to David on the couch.

Then it occurred to her as she sat across from David that

they were the only two people, besides Anne, who were not part of a couple. Intentionally or unintentionally, she had a feeling they were being paired up. She supposed she didn't mind. She liked David well enough. He was handsome, even without the new haircut and beard. She had always been drawn to smart men. Her last serious relationship had been with a university professor. David, as a chemist, might be a different kind of smart, but he was an intelligent man. She'd spent enough time in his lab to know he was very hands-on and had ultimate approval of every product Brown sold.

Anne passed Juliet a bowl of mashed potatoes. "How are you enjoying America, Juliet?"

Juliet accepted the bowl with a smile. "I like it well enough. The weather here in California is a sight better than London. But America, what I've seen of it anyway, is different and it's taking me a little while to get used to the pace. I'm still not sure about purchasing a car and driving on the other side of the road. Back home, it was easier to take public transport, so it has been a while since I've driven."

Sebastian gave Juliet a sympathetic look. "I felt the same when I arrived in London. It took me a while to settle in. And then trying to figure out the words for things was a challenge."

"I remember a few blunders you made. I imagine I'll make a few here. But I've worked with people from around the globe, so I got used to speaking using words that most people would understand."

Anne took the bowl when Juliet handed it back to her. "It must be hard to be away from your family."

Juliet found her gaze on David's instead of Anne's. "I don't have family. My parents both passed when I was in my early twenties, and I was an only child. They were a bit older when they had me, and they both took ill in their sixties. I suppose there might be some relatives out there, but my parents never spoke of them."

Anne patted her hand. "I didn't have a family of my own until I married Howard. Now I have a large one."

David smirked at Juliet. "Want to marry me and join the

family?"

Juliet choked on her sip of wine and took a moment to compose herself. "That's quite the offer, David. I'll think about it."

David's smirk turned into a scowl.

Anne laughed. "Well, Juliet, I suppose you could do worse than David. But you'd have to polish some of his rough edges first."

Juliet gave David a self-satisfied smile. "I got the hair and beard polished. A new wardrobe, and a personality adjustment, and he'll be perfect husband material."

Teasing went around the room at that comment, each person having an idea of how Juliet could turn David into the perfect husband. Leslie, being his sister, had more than a few ideas to share.

David stopped scowling at some point and found the humor in the situation. Instead of retaliating and offering suggestions that would make Juliet his ideal wife, he kept quiet. He supposed he deserved the comments after his tongue-in-cheek proposal.

The rest of the evening was a raucous one. The children played, and the adults continued to laugh and tease over dessert and a glass of sherry. It was almost midnight by the time Juliet was ready to say her goodbyes.

Sebastian motioned for David. "Can you take Juliet home? I don't want her to take a cab this late at night."

David gave his keys a toss. "Sure. Let me get my jacket."

Juliet said her goodbyes to the family, thanking them for their hospitality and including her in their holiday celebration. Within moments, she found herself in David's car.

Juliet gave him her address and directed him to the highway. "Nice car. It's not what I expected."

David glanced over at Juliet, the dash lights highlighting her cheekbones. "I suppose you expected something flashy."

Juliet nodded. The sedate car was nice. It probably cost him a small fortune, but she would have pegged him for the type who drove a sportier car, one that would impress the ladies. "That wasn't an insult."

David turned onto the highway. "Didn't take it that way. I like legroom, so a sports car was out, but I didn't want a huge SUV either. This is easier to park in the city."

She changed the subject. "You have a nice family. Everyone seems to get along."

David glanced her way. "We didn't always. Evelyn and I used to fight a lot. We've mellowed as we've gotten older. And Sebastian and Anne are nice buffers and keep us from going too far. Leslie and I used to fight a lot, too, but Leslie, well, she's a whole different person since she got married and had a kid. She's been harping on me to find the perfect woman and settle down."

"Rumors are you aren't interested in those types of relationships."

David didn't deny the rumors. "No, I haven't been interested in those types of relationships. And none of the women I've dated have been able to change my mind."

That piqued Juliet's interest. "So if you found a woman

who could change your mind about marriage and permanency, you'd be interested in that kind of relationship?"

"Why, are you interested?"

Juliet folded her hands in her lap and kept her eyes on the road in front of her. "You did propose earlier."

David glanced at her but couldn't read her expression. "I suppose I should apologize for that, but you didn't answer my question."

Juliet shrugged. "I'm not interested in being one in a long string of women."

"That's straightforward enough."

Juliet shifted slightly towards him. "Look. You're an attractive man. You're single. And I'll admit I've been a little lonely. I've been working so much since I arrived; I've barely had more than a few hours that I haven't been working. My weekends have been spent putting plans in motion. But let's just say going out once in a while with a man would be nice. Maybe dinner and a little dancing."

David scowled. "Sorry, I don't dance."

"Dinner then?"

David's scowl turned into a gape. "Are you asking me out?"

Juliet nodded. "Just dinner and some conversation. I'm not asking you to marry me. And I'm not asking you to give up those other women. I think we could be friends."

David pulled into the parking lot of Juliet's apartment building. "I don't have female friends. But I suppose we could give it a try."

Juliet released the seat belt before leaning over and kissing David's cheek. "It's settled. How about Saturday if you're not busy?"

David thought of the woman he was taking to dinner on Saturday. She was tall, had long black hair that fell to her waist, and had a body he'd been aching to get his hands on. "Saturday is no good. How about Sunday? We can have an early dinner."

She noticed the look on his face and some of Juliet's

enthusiasm waned, but she nodded. "How about you pick me up at five?"

David jotted down her apartment number. Since he parked in front of her building, and because there was a doorman, he didn't bother to offer to walk her up. "I'll see you Sunday."

Juliet nodded and closed the door. She greeted the doorman by name before heading to the elevators. Her heart was pounding in her chest. What had she been thinking, asking David out? Yes, she was a bit lonely. Having dinner with Sebastian's family had driven home how lonely she had been feeling since she arrived. And she was serious when she told David she hadn't had much time to get out and meet people. She'd been constantly on the move since she arrived, trying to fix Brown's problems. And she was confident her ideas would work. But now that she was implementing them, she wouldn't have to work quite so hard. And with the long holiday weekend looming before her, she'd let her emotions get the better of her.

David's proposal had also set her heart to pounding. She knew he wasn't serious, but a seed had been planted and it had been tickling her subconscious all evening. She could admit to being attracted to David. She already had, though she hadn't thought much of it, certainly not enough to contemplate asking him out on a date. She was not David's type, of that she was certain. She heard enough rumors around the office to know what his type was. But friendship was nice and safe, and it wouldn't hurt to get her feet wet in the dating world again. It had been a long time since her last relationship had fallen apart. She hadn't been eager to have it happen again. But if she just remembered David wasn't a permanent kind of man, and that it was just dinner between friends, she could handle it.

Chapter Four

David spent Friday night in the lab. It wasn't unusual for him to go in when no one else was around. He'd spotted Juliet leaving the building as he was heading in, but he'd ducked into a hallway so she wouldn't see him. He had watched her from the shadows as she made notations on her ever-present tablet. But what grabbed his attention was her legs. Instead of wearing a suit with a skirt and jacket, she had worn a pair of jeans that hugged her legs and accentuated her curvy bottom. The oversized t-shirt wasn't enough to hide her curves.

She was attractive. He could admit it. But he didn't like her. And he still wasn't sure what possessed him to accept her dinner invitation, even as just friends.

Saturday, he spent his morning doing much of the same, working on his newest product line. When Saturday evening came around, he and his date had gone to a local hot spot. The date had started off well enough. They'd flirted over cocktails and conversation. But as dinner wore on, his mind had started to drift. His date's inane chatter had become irritating, and he'd become distracted thinking about his dinner with Juliet the next evening. He had realized he hadn't yet decided where to take her. She said dinner and dancing, but he'd meant what he said. He didn't dance. He'd been known to sway with a pretty woman now and again, but that was the limit of his dancing skills.

What irritated him the most was that he went home alone. And by choice. His date with the long black hair and luscious body hadn't been enough to distract him from his thoughts of Juliet. When he'd kissed his date in the hallway outside her apartment door, he couldn't drum up the desire to take her to bed. She had been more than willing and had been angry with him when he'd instead bid her goodnight.

He'd blown whatever chance he'd had with her.

By the time he was ready to pick Juliet up for their dinner date, he was frustrated and angry with her. She was the reason he'd spent last night in his own bed. It was her lips he had wanted to kiss; her body he had wanted to touch.

Juliet opened her door before David knocked on it. She smiled briefly at him but had her back to him as she locked her door, so she missed his scowl. "I hope you have someplace in mind for dinner. I've eaten at the diner down the road, but I wouldn't recommend it."

David stuffed his hands in his pockets in a bid to keep his hands off her hair. "Italian, Chinese, Indian, Tai, Mexican? Lady's choice."

Juliet tucked her keys in her bag and turned to face David. Her smile faded. "Something wrong?"

Something was wrong, but he didn't want to admit it to her. She had a dress on; the flowy skirt of this one went just past her knees. Her feet and ankles looked delicate in the tiny sandals she wore. The wine color of her dress brought out the gold in her skin. The draping left little to the imagination. The fabric hugged her breasts and nipped in her waist. Her hair looked soft and wavy as it lay loose around her shoulders.

"David?" Juliet looked down to make sure everything was in place.

David snapped out of it. "Everything's fine. Let's do Mexican."

Juliet let David take her hand but had to trot to keep up with him. "Are we in a hurry?"

Thankfully, they were at his car, and he didn't have to answer the question. He opened the door for her. He ignored her quizzical look and shut the door as soon as her feet were in.

"I haven't had a lot of Mexican food, though there are plenty of places to eat it in London, but I tried a small place a couple of weeks ago not far from my flat. I liked the spiciness of it."

David made some sort of reply, and it seemed to satisfy

her. He replied to her conversation in mostly one- or two-word answers, keeping his focus on the road.

Juliet shifted uncomfortably in her seat. She had a feeling she'd made a mistake asking David out. But not one to give up easily, she kept up her one-sided conversation. The restaurant he'd selected was nice, and the people friendly. She chatted briefly with their hostess, who was curious about her accent. She then had a lengthy conversation with their waiter on what to order. She would have asked David, but he had his unapproachable face on. She'd gotten quite used to that face in the months since she'd started working at Brown.

"Take it your date didn't go well last night?" Juliet took a bite of the crispy tortilla chip, quickly swallowing a drink of water when the heat of the salsa was too much for her taste buds.

David dipped a chip and took a bite. He'd ordered the extra spicy salsa, and Juliet looked like she might choke from the heat of it. Feeling oddly satisfied, he took another bite.

"Went just fine. I took her to a local club. Had dinner and drinks."

Juliet dropped her gaze. She knew his reputation and imagined he'd spent the night with the woman he'd been so keen to go out with. "So why didn't we go to a club?"

David took a sip of his tequila. "I only take dates there."

"And I'm not a date."

"Just friends, though I'm not sure I'd call us that either."

He was baiting her; she just couldn't figure out why. She'd been looking forward to spending some time with him outside of work. Obviously, she'd made a mistake. "No, I guess we're not."

Conversation was stilted through dinner. Juliet no longer had hopes of their being friends. In fact, he was doing everything in his power to be rude. In the course of a twenty-minute meal, he'd managed to mock her work, mock her campaign, and make her feel like the most unattractive woman in the room.

After that, Juliet had had enough. She excused herself to

go to the ladies' room.

David swallowed the last of his tequila, cursing himself. He'd just been the biggest ass, and he knew it. He owed her an apology. A big one. He just didn't have an explanation. Yes, he was frustrated. He hadn't expected to find himself this attracted to Juliet. But it was hardly her fault he hadn't taken his date to bed last night. It wasn't her fault that their dinner was a disaster.

He was starting to get worried when their waiter came. "What?"

"The lady said to have a nice night." The waiter set a glass of tequila on the table.

It took a moment, then it dawned on him that she'd left. "I'll take the bill."

"Lady paid it. I know it's none of my business, but that was one classy lady you ticked off."

David scowled, leaving the drink untouched on the table. He grabbed his jacket and left.

When he got outside, he looked around but didn't see her.

It seemed unlikely she'd been able to find a cab conveniently waiting for a fare. And she couldn't have gotten far in her sandals. But after driving around the surrounding streets, he saw no sign of her. He pulled out his cell, then realized he didn't have her number. Cursing himself and her, he tossed the phone down and did what he always did when he needed to think. He went to his lab.

The offices of Brown Chemicals were dark. He waved to the security officer who was not at all surprised to see him. He headed straight to his lab and took a seat at his desk. His desk was a lab table filled with papers covered in various notes, chemical symbols, and even an occasional doodle. But instead of settling in, he went to his office where the hated computer sat. He spent very little time in his office, preferring the noise and familiarity of the lab when he worked. He quickly accessed the personnel files. While he might hate the computer, he did know how to use one.

He found Juliet's phone number but hesitated to call it. He doubted his call would be well received. But he was worried and wanted to at least make sure she'd made it home. With renewed determination, he dialed. He was surprised when she answered.

"Go to bed, David. I'll see you tomorrow."

David heard the line drop as quickly as it had picked up. He didn't realize she had his number. Or that she'd have it programmed in her phone.

He dropped down on the couch alongside the wall. It was another spot he didn't spend much time. He was known to sleep at the office from time to time, usually passed out at his desk, and he always kept a fresh change of clothes on hand. Doing as he was told, David stretched out and dropped off to sleep.

Chapter Five

"First things first, we need to clean up this mess. I see David didn't." Juliet, her tablet clutched to her chest, directed the crew to set up lighting for the test shots. She once again wished the office had not been closed Friday. She was already behind as it was. And after the fiasco of a dinner date last night with David, she just wanted to get the shots over with and clear out of his space.

"Yes, Ms. Torrance." The eager assistant had brought a couple of boxes with her, as instructed.

"Just don't mess them up, or their order. Mr. Bennett will have our heads."

"He'll have more than that." David scowled at the people invading his lab. He might have agreed to this, but that didn't mean he had to be gracious about it.

Juliet raised a brow at his appearance. "Good thing I brought help. You look quite disheveled this morning. Donna can hopefully make you presentable. Why don't you get washed up first?"

David noticed that most of the people in the room were watching them. "Why don't you help me?"

Juliet was about to protest, but the look on David's face stopped her. Instead, she dealt out a few more assignments before following David out of the room. She closed the door of his office behind them as he headed to his private bath. "Want to apologize to me for last night?"

He had, but not when she had that superior air about her. He hated it when she came into his space and acted like he was the one inconveniencing her. "It was your idea."

Juliet set her tablet on his unused desk. "Not one of my better ones. You cured me, David. I won't ask again."

David grunted at that and shut the bathroom door.

Juliet sat down on the couch. He had hurt her yesterday,

though she doubted he even realized it. She enjoyed sparring with him, but she'd hoped that maybe their relationship could have become something less adversarial. She hadn't been sure she wanted more than friendship from him, but after last night, she realized she'd been fooling herself. She had been looking for something more intimate with him than friendship. Dinner would have been a nice first step in feeling her way around this attraction she felt towards him. He'd certainly dashed that hope.

David opened the bathroom door, his face scrubbed and his beard trimmed. There wasn't much he could do about his hair at the moment, other than wet it down. He wasn't about to take a shower with a crew full of people in his lab.

Juliet snatched her tablet from the desk. "I have a new lab coat for you, but it hasn't arrived yet. That tattered thing you wear is on its last leg. Donna brought some clothes for you to try. I like your slacks, but your shirts need work. She also brought in some new shoes. They haven't fared better than your jacket."

David strode towards her. "I'm starting to feel like Pygmalion's statue. Trying to turn me into your perfect man?"

"Hardly. Though you do have a hard head. But I date scholarly types. And while you're smart, I wouldn't call you a scholar."

David took a step closer. "You're calling me hard-headed?"

Juliet once again clutched her tablet to her chest. "After dinner last night, I have a few other words to describe you, but I like to think of myself as a lady. A lady wouldn't use those words in public."

David could imagine what some of those words were. "What if I said I was sorry?"

Juliet narrowed her eyes and found herself taking a step backward. "I don't know, since you haven't actually apologized. But I guess my question to you is why?"

David took the tablet from her and tossed it on the seat she'd vacated. "It started on Saturday night. I had a hot date.

I took her to the club. I plied her with drinks. And I was bored in less than half an hour. We finished dinner, had another drink, and I took her home. I kissed that luscious mouth, molded those curves with my hands, and you know what happened next?"

Juliet knew exactly what had happened next. "I don't need an anatomy lesson, David. I'm a grown woman. And you are free to do what you want with whomever you want."

David took a step closer and got immense satisfaction when her eyes widened. "I'll tell you what happened. Nothing. I went home alone. You want to know why?"

Unable to get a word out through the constriction in her throat, she felt herself nodding.

David pressed Juliet up against the wall, his arms trapping her. "I thought of you. I wanted to kiss you. To touch you. Not her."

Juliet wet her lips, but whatever words might have formed faded under the force of his kiss. Her hands came up to clench his biceps, and she was not at all surprised by the steely strength in them. He might be a chemist who practically lived in his lab, but he managed to find time to keep in shape. Instead of pulling away as she knew she should, she used his strength to bring her mouth closer, her lips and tongue joining in the frenzy of his kiss.

David's hands drifted down to settle at her waist, bringing her body flush with his. He felt her arms wrap around his neck, and he used the opportunity to lift her and settle her on the couch. Not caring where they were or that there were people just outside the door, he settled on top of her, his hands now anchoring her face so he could devour her mouth. The sweet, hot flavor of her went straight to his head, and the blood pulsing in his veins headed south.

Juliet heard the moan in the back of her throat, but instead of doing the logical thing, she wound her fingers into his hair and held on. He kissed her like he was starving. And perhaps after leaving his last date at her door, he was. Despite that thought, she returned the kiss with the same fervor.

A loud knock on the door had David cursing and pulling away from Juliet. Her skirt had ridden up, and he could see the pink satin underwear she was wearing. Groaning, he turned away from her. He poked his head out of his door to see Evelyn standing there.

"What?"

Evelyn, used to his surly ways, ignored his tone. "I'm looking for Juliet. The package she was waiting for was delivered, so I thought I'd bring it over and see the lab. It's not every day we have a film crew hanging out."

Juliet closed her eyes for a moment before sitting up. She straightened her skirt, and her hair felt okay, but she had a feeling she looked like a woman who had been making out on the sofa with the boss's cousin. Strumming up what little was left of her professionalism, she came around David so she could speak to Evelyn.

Juliet took the box, ignoring the question on her employer's face. "Thanks. This has to be the new lab coat. I had to special order it."

David took the box when it was shoved into his hands. He looked at the shipping label. It was from the company he liked to shop at when it was time for new equipment or a new coat. He saw Juliet smiling at him.

Juliet knew what he was thinking. "I asked. Go ahead and try it on. It probably will need to be pressed. But Donna will take care of that."

Juliet started to follow Evelyn back into the lab, away from David.

David called after her, waving her tablet. When she got close enough to take it, he leaned in so only she could hear him. "We're not finished."

Juliet snatched her tablet from his hands. "I need to get to work."

David let her go, unsure if his words were a threat or a promise. He supposed it didn't matter. The outcome would be the same. He'd had a taste, and now he wanted more.

Chapter Six

David wasn't sure how she managed it, but Juliet was able to make sure the two of them were not alone together. There had been no repeat of the kiss in his office. There had been no requests for dinner dates. She was back to the Juliet he knew so well, the one who flitted in and out of his lab, made a nuisance of herself, and was forever making notes.

He'd have been upset about it, but he could feel the tension in the room when she came in. And he would catch her looking at him through her lashes. He knew she wasn't immune, and that gave him a measure of satisfaction.

But right now, he had bigger problems. Today they were filming his marketing segment. He'd been given a script to use to talk to an imaginary audience about the company and the products he developed. He had spent the last two nights going over the script, and he could barely remember any of it. The pretty red-haired assistant was off to the side writing up cue cards for him. It was humiliating.

He'd sat through test shots three days before and had to endure feeling like an idiot while he'd been groomed, had makeup applied in layers to his face, and said stupid things to a camera to see how photogenic he was and how he came across on film. From what he could tell, the film director, the photographer, the stylist, and Juliet were pleased with what they saw.

Juliet handed David a cup of coffee. "It's not that bad, you know. You're going to look great on camera, and the first of our media campaigns will be ready next week in time for Christmas. Think of all those people using your beauty products and using your cleaning supplies, getting ready for Christmas parties and Christmas dinners."

David gratefully took the coffee. He took a swallow and realized it was made exactly as he liked it. He frowned down at it.

Juliet took the frown as a bad sign. "Look. You'll have the cards. All you have to do is talk about the product like you do in project meetings. You have so much enthusiasm for what you do that it will show."

David took another swallow. "Let's just get this over with."

It wasn't as bad as he had been imagining it. Juliet stood behind the camera; her smile and her approval helped boost his confidence. And she was right. He didn't have to fake enthusiasm when it came to the products he carefully developed. Time flew by, and before he knew it, the director called it a wrap.

Juliet clapped when the filming was over. "David, that was amazing. Thank you, everyone. You can have your lab back."

That garnered a few cheers from the lab staff. They'd been working around the lighting fixtures and in cramped spaces since the furniture had been moved around to accommodate a set.

David watched as Juliet thanked each person in turn while the efficient film crew packed up the equipment.

Once the room was mostly empty and the furniture back in its place, Juliet sought out David. "We may need a few more photos, but overall, I'm pleased. You're now off the hook. I've got the crew heading over to the boardroom to set up to film Sebastian and Evelyn. I may even get little Brittany worked into the script."

David took Juliet's hand. "Have dinner with me."

Juliet sighed. "I'm not sure that's a good idea, David. You seem to have only two speeds. Stop and warp speed."

David's thumb stroked her inner wrist. "I'm sure I can find a speed somewhere in the middle."

Juliet was afraid that even in the middle, things were going too fast. She also feared she would find herself alone for the ride. He might hop into her lane for a time, but he'd eventually speed off to the next woman. She'd already had her heart broken once. She wasn't too keen to try again.

"Juliet?"

She looked up into David's eyes. She had a feeling she was about to make the biggest mistake of her life. "Dinner. Saturday. I'm too busy the rest of the week. And I'm spending Friday evening with your cousins and sister."

David dropped her hand. He'd heard rumors about a girl's night at Kimberly's house. He could wait. "Saturday."

* * *

Juliet enjoyed the Bennett clan. Evelyn might be her boss, but she had invited her to her sister Kimberly's house for girl's night. Juliet was grateful for the invite. And the laughter from the women was catching.

"Speaking of men, what is going on between you and David?" Evelyn was relaxed in a lounge chair by the pool, her body draped in a towel. Juliet knew Evelyn had terrible scars on her legs and was self-conscious about them. Juliet had been horrified when she learned that an ex-employee of

Brown had tried to kill her a few years back.

"What relationship?" This came from Leslie, David's sister.

"No relationship. We had dinner once, and it was a disaster."

Evelyn took a sip of her drink. "Looked to me like you two made up."

Juliet flushed under the three pairs of eyes watching her. "Look, we kissed; no big deal."

Leslie stat forward. "I don't suppose you're serious about him, are you? I don't know if I can handle any more family events with those women he brings. I keep saying he needs an intelligent woman who can keep him on his toes."

Juliet supposed she should be flattered at not being lumped in with his less-than-brilliant girlfriends, but she was uncomfortable talking about it. Her feelings for him were so jumbled, and she wasn't going to have them sorted out by their dinner date tomorrow.

As she sat there, she realized the women were not going

to let it go. They were all staring at her waiting. "Fine. We're having dinner tomorrow."

Leslie smiled. "That makes two. By three you'll either be done or ready to walk down the aisle. David never makes it past three. Of course, before I got married, I never did either."

Juliet heard the involuntary question pop out of her mouth. "Why?"

Leslie shrugged. "Our parents got divorced when we were both young. And before that, they were not faithful to each other. In fact, they seemed to thrive trying to one-up the other. We ended up living with our mother, and our dad was rarely around. And my mom wasn't what you'd call family-oriented. Guess neither our parents nor Evelyn and Kimberly's parents were. David dates for a while, then stops. Then he repeats the pattern. I suppose for him the time he spends in his lab occupies so much of his time that he hasn't been interested in pursuing a serious relationship."

Juliet's experience was the opposite. While her parents

were older than most of her friend's parents, they had been devoted to each other. Rarely were harsh words spoken in her childhood home. And she would bet neither had ever contemplated being unfaithful.

Juliet thought about what Leslie said most of the night and into the next day. When David knocked on her door, she still hadn't sorted out her feelings.

Chapter Seven

Determined to do this right this time, David showed up on Juliet's doorstep promptly at five with pink roses in hand.

Juliet took the roses, inhaled their scent, and gestured for David to come in. "They're beautiful."

David wanted to say not as beautiful as she was but refrained. It would sound like a line, and a bad one at that. But she was beautiful. Tonight, she was wearing a pair of linen slacks and a blouse tied at the waist. Her feet were bare, and her hair was up in a loose twist.

Juliet returned to the living room space with the roses in a vase. "I'm glad I picked this up. I was at a shop that had handblown glassware, and I just couldn't resist the aqua shades in this piece. I got rid of most of my things when I came."

David cleared his throat. He was suddenly struggling for words. "Where do you want to eat tonight?"

Juliet set the vase on a side table, fluffed the flowers, and turned back to David. "I cooked. That way, if you get out of hand, I can simply throw you out and not have to catch a bus home."

David felt himself flush. "I wondered how you got home. I looked for you. I was a jerk."

Juliet tipped her head and contemplated him for a moment. "I guess I'm still unsure why. But we'll set that aside for tonight. Come join me."

David followed her to her small kitchen. There wasn't much space, but she'd managed to fit in a small bistro table and chairs, and dinner was served on a rollaway cart.

David glanced suspiciously at the cart of food. "What are we having?"

Juliet set two plates on the table and dished up a green salad before scooping a potato and fish mixture onto his plate. "It's fish pie. Just try it."

David took a seat and continued to eye the food. "What if I don't like fish?"

Juliet poured them both a glass of chardonnay. "You like fish."

David shrugged and took a bite. He took a second. "This is good. How do you know I like fish?"

Juliet dropped her head so he wouldn't see her self-satisfied smile. "Your sister told me."

David had forgotten about girls' night. "Besides the fact that I like fish, what else did she tell you?"

Juliet took a sip of her wine, savoring the flavor. "She told me about your parents. I'm sorry you had to go through that. My parents were great. I still miss them terribly."

David set a hand on top of hers. He might not be happy Leslie spoke about their parents to her, but he sympathized with her loss. "You mentioned them at Thanksgiving. You didn't say much else other than that they were gone. I don't know much about you."

She turned her palm up and squeezed his hand before drawing it to her lap. "We never got around to talking about ourselves at our last dinner."

He had earned that remark and leaned back in his chair. "So what do I need to know about Juliet? Besides that she lived in London and has a sexy accent."

Juliet struggled not to smile but lost. "Not a lot to know, really. I was born and raised in London. My work here for Brown is the first time I've been to the United States. I'm enjoying California despite the smog, and despite a rough start, I'm enjoying dinner with you tonight."

David was not satisfied with her answer, though he took it as a good sign she would admit to enjoying dinner. "That's an awfully brief autobiography. Were you seeing anyone before you came here?"

Juliet took another sip of her wine before answering. She knew what he really was asking her. "Not when I left. But before. I came close to getting engaged. He was a professor at Queen Mary University. We spent three years together.

And then I found out he was having an affair with a grad student. Our engagement didn't happen, and I moved on. When Sebastian asked me to come, it seemed like the change I was looking for. As you can imagine, with your reputation, you are not the man I would have thought to invite to dinner. But beneath your scowl lies a man who knows what he wants in life and is passionate about what he does. Those traits are ones I admire in a man. Is that what you were hoping to hear?"

David was still reeling a little. He'd been thrown by the word engaged. Had her professor not been a cheating jerk, he'd never have met her. "Yes, I guess that is sort of what I was hoping to hear. But I didn't expect you to be quite so honest."

Juliet didn't like games and wasn't one to mince words, at least not in her personal life. Given that she worked in marketing and public relations, some games were unavoidable. "David, I like you. I'm attracted to you. But I don't think you like me. Attracted maybe, but you find me a nuisance."

That was true, and she still annoyed him at work, but outside of work, he was finding differently. "Maybe I just don't like P.R. Juliet. I'm finding the real you a lot more fascinating."

Juliet poured them both another glass of wine. "I suppose 'fascinating' might be a good place to start. But then again, people find sharks and snakes fascinating, too."

David wiped his mouth with the napkin she'd set out and rose. He touched a lock of her hair. "Why don't we find out?"

Juliet set the bottle down and let David kiss her. His fingers stroked her neck, and this kiss was softer, less urgent than the one in his office.

David lifted his head. "I'd say I like the real Juliet very much."

Juliet didn't try to fight the allure of his kiss. When he bent his head back to her, she wrapped her arms around his neck and found her hands in his hair. His kisses drew her deeper and deeper until she had no desire to protest his advances.

David couldn't get enough of her taste. Her soft hands caressed his scalp, and he couldn't resist returning the favor.

"David?" Juliet tipped her head to the side to give him access to her neck.

"I love the way you say my name. Juliet, let me take you to bed."

Juliet figured she had two choices. She could say no, and most likely find herself in exactly this same spot again, assuming they made it to dinner number three. Or she could give in to the inevitable and say yes. She figured no matter her answer, she was in for another heartache. She knew it was not likely there would be a future with him, but how could she be sure unless she took a risk? In the end, she found she couldn't say no.

Decision made, Juliet led David to her bedroom. It was early yet, the sunset in its early stages. She pulled the blinds so no one could see in, but they blocked very little light. The room was dim, but she was able to see the desire on David's face. For tonight, it would be enough.

David remembered her words to him about only having two speeds. But while he wasn't about to put the brakes on, he could at least not rush her. He leisurely kissed her, taking his time stripping off her clothes one piece at a time, taking time between the removal of each piece to appreciate what he had uncovered. Her body was slim and curvy, and she fit against his body perfectly.

Juliet returned the favor, savoring this time with him, much as she had done with her wine. She lingered over each kiss, each touch. And she was moved by the care he was showing her, not rushing to the finish.

But Juliet wasn't satisfied for long. She pulled him down on the bed with her, enjoying the weight of his body on top of hers. She kissed him, this time more urgently, and he took the hint.

David made a feast of her, needing the feel of her thighs tightening around his hips, arching her back to give him better access to her breasts. And when he finally surged into her, they both cried out at the pleasure of it. Making love to Juliet was unlike any experience he'd had. She moved in time with him, her nails dug into his back, and her body gripped him as if she never wanted to let go.

And when Juliet climaxed in his arms, he cherished every moment before letting go.

Chapter Eight

Juliet decided she wasn't going to question David or ask for more than he wanted to give. But for the next two weeks, they were rarely apart, and Juliet was happy. They made it to a third dinner, a fourth, and beyond. Some nights they ate out and others they ate in. And while, despite Leslie's prediction, they were not on the verge of marriage, David had taken to spending most nights at her flat. He'd kiss her and sneak out early, heading to his condo to shower and change. Personally, she was simply happy and glad that David wanted to spend time with her.

She was dangerously close to falling in love with him. She could admit that, at least to herself. When they weren't working, David was a wonderful companion. They talked about movies, art, music, and history. He expressed interest in seeing London one day, and while she didn't offer to show it to him, she would love to show him her hometown, her history.

Professionally, she supposed she should not have expected any changes there. He was not thrilled with the ad campaign. He said they made him feel like an idiot. But she thought they were great. He had a presence on camera that few amateurs had. Had he any desire, he'd have made quite the splash in television or movies.

But more importantly, Evelyn and Sebastian were happy with the campaigns. Sales were up, press had been positive, and the company's message of caring about the ingredients and chemicals that were used in their products resonated with audiences. Sebastian was asked for interviews with different media outlets, and Juliet oversaw them. David had been asked for a few, but he had vehemently declined. As far as he was concerned, he'd done his duty.

But tonight was the next step in her media blitz. She'd

reserved a room at a nearby hotel for a dinner party with the city's business and political elite. David had grumbled, more than grumbled, but had finally agreed to attend, but only because she told him she needed an escort. At first, he had refused, but when she said she'd have to find someone else then, he'd agreed. He argued with her about manipulating him into it, but eventually, he'd dropped the subject with a promise he'd get his tux dry-cleaned for the event.

So here she was on a Saturday evening, wearing a lovely silver and blue dress she'd found at a specialty boutique, escorted by her lover. "The hotel did a fantastic job."

David tugged at his bow tie. "Looks good. But I expected nothing less from you. Let's just get this over with."

Juliet frowned at his tone but decided not to press her luck and start an argument.

David mostly behaved himself, so Juliet was grateful. But halfway through the party, she was introduced to one of David's ex-girlfriends, who was the guest of one of the local businessmen who had been invited. Unable to take any more of the woman's catty comments and lustful stares, she excused herself and left David with Evelyn and Sebastian, as well as his ex.

Other women came and went from the ladies' room, but Juliet needed a few moments alone and paid them no mind. She supposed it was inevitable she'd come face to face with one of David's girlfriends. And from the woman's comments and tone, they hadn't been just friends. Vivica Armstrong was stunning. She was tall, almost as tall as David, and had long black hair and the brightest blue eyes Juliet had ever seen. In comparison to the raven beauty, Juliet felt like second prize.

In that moment, Juliet knew she wasn't just falling in love with David; she was already in love with David. And what was she doing, leaving him alone with that woman? Juliet squared her shoulders, adjusted her cleavage to display it as best she could, freshened her lipstick, and stalked back into the party, a woman determined to rescue her man from the clutches of a raven who couldn't possibly love or appreciate him the way she did.

She glanced around and saw Evelyn and Sebastian, but no David. She waved away Sebastian's questioning gaze and looked for David in the crowd. When she couldn't find him, she went out to the terrace where a few couples were dancing, and others were simply enjoying each other's company.

Juliet was about to give up when she heard a laugh from behind her. Not far from the terrace doorway was a darkened space. Dreading what she feared most, she made her way to the couple. She didn't realize she had made a sound until David pushed Vivica away from him. The woman clung to him like a limpet. Even in the faint light, she could clearly see Vivica's red lipstick on David's mouth.

Without a word, Juliet turned and fled the terrace. She was aware that the other couples knew what had just transpired, but she didn't care. She just wanted to get out of there. Thankfully she had her purse and keys and didn't need to fetch them from the coat check counter.

"Juliet!" David's shout could be heard over the crowd, but most people ignored it and continued their conversations, enjoying the free food and drinks.

Juliet debated whether to try to make it to her car without him catching up to her or to duck through the nearby door. She chose the door. The room was dark and mostly empty, except for a few tables and chairs stored away. She was looking for another exit when the door swung open.

David didn't bother to close the door behind him but stalked over to where Juliet stood. He could see her shoulders trembling, and he was afraid those were tears in her eyes. He cursed himself and then cursed Vivica. And for good measure, he cursed the fates that had her at this party. Vivica, with the long black hair and luscious lips. But just as when he took her to dinner, and just as before when he'd kissed her, she didn't stir him.

"It's not what you think, Juliet."

Juliet gave an unladylike snort at that. "No, of course

not. I guess when I said you could date other women, I should have clarified that the deal was off if you were sleeping with me."

David took a step closer and took her hand. She didn't fight him, which worried him more than if she'd tried to hit him. "It wasn't what it looked like. I was only out there with her because she was trying to pick a fight, and I didn't want to embarrass you or the family."

"Of course, I forgot. You always kiss women when you're trying to stop a fight. It worked on me in your office, so why not on her too."

David clasped her to him. "I kissed you because I wanted you. She kissed me. I didn't kiss her."

Juliet pulled away. "Right. Next you're going to tell me you didn't sleep with her."

David wiped a tear that streamed down her cheek. "Remember after our first dinner? Remember when I told you about my date? The one I had kissed, touched, and then left at her door? Vivica was that woman. And do you remember why I didn't sleep with her?"

Juliet's words were soft. "You said you wanted to kiss me. That you wanted me."

David pulled her to him again, this time wrapping his arms around her waist. "That's right. I wanted you. I still want you. I'll want you every day for the rest of my life. I want to marry you. Before I couldn't figure out why I passed up my chance with her. But I know now. I love you, Juliet."

Juliet remained still, her body stiff, her eyes on his. She then released her breath and relaxed in his arms. Fresh tears fell, but these were different. "I love you, David."

David let out his own breath and pulled her closer, her face buried in his chest. He wanted to kiss her, but he wasn't yet ready to release his hold on her. "Marry me?"

Juliet shifted so her cheek lay on his shoulder, her arms around his neck, holding on with all her strength. "I'll have to tell Leslie it was fifteen."

David had no clue what she was talking about. He shifted her so he could see her face, but didn't ease his hold on her. "Fifteen what?"

She kissed the underside of his chin. "Fifteen dinners. I've been counting. She said it would only take three dinners before you proposed or broke up with me. It took you fifteen to propose."

David tipped her face up to his so he could lightly kiss her between words. "So I'm an idiot. I should have proposed during our first dinner."

She pulled back and smiled up at him. "Technically our first dinner together was Thanksgiving dinner, and if I recall, you did propose."

He grinned and swept her up in his arms. "You didn't say yes then. How about now? Will you marry me, Juliet?"

She cupped his face in her palm. "Yes."

Cheers rose up from the open doorway. David turned, still holding Juliet, to see his sister, Evelyn, and Sebastian beaming at them.

Leslie spoke for the crowd. "It's about time. Welcome, Juliet, to the Bennett clan."

Juliet looked up at David, her love plain for all to see. Then she sealed their engagement with a passionate kiss right there in front of her soon-to-be family.

From The Author

I hope you enjoyed reading A Bride For David. David was a secondary character in my novel This Time Love. I never intended for the story, or the characters, to go beyond that book. And though I like reading novellas, I never thought I'd write one. I'm not sure when the idea to write David's story popped into my mind, but ultimately his story took root. I like Juliet for him, a woman who knows her mind, knows what she wants, and works to get it. And she's smart enough to give David a run for his money.

If you enjoyed the book and would like an email on my next release, you can sign up at my website @elizabeth-castle.com/contact. Please be assured your email will never be. You can also follow me on Facebook @ facebook.com/elizabethcastle.romanceauthor

Also, if you enjoyed this book, or any of my other titles, please consider leaving a rating at your favorite retailer, Goodreads and/or Bookbub. And if you have the time, a text review would be lovely. Indie authors rely on readers like you to tell others how much you enjoy their books.

Happy reading,

Books by Elizabeth Castle

Single Titles:
    Going Home
    This Kind Of Love
    Chasing Hope
    The Babe & The Librarian (novella)

The Heart's Way Series:
    For Now and Always
    Ask Me To
    Say You Love Me
    Forever Love

Bennett Family Series:
    This Time Love
    A Bride For David
(novella)

All Of Me Series:
    All Of My Days
    All Of My Nights

Cantwell Quartet:
    Falling Slowly
    Unraveled
    Hidden Away
    Entangled

Contemporary "Retro" Romance Series:
    Loving Jordan

Visit elizabeth-castle.com for newsletter sign up and up-to-date releases.

Excerpt From This Time Love

Chapter One

The bedroom was done in soothing sage greens with accents of bright orchid pink. When the sun came up in the morning, light filtered through the gauzy cream-colored curtains, easing her into wakefulness. The sanctuary feel of the room had been purposefully created with the help of her family. It was supposed to be relaxing and calming. The fresh flowers decorating the low table and dresser were supposed to appeal to her senses.

Nothing in the room could calm her today.

Evelyn Bennett refused to humiliate herself again. Her grandfather had called it "her cussed stubbornness," but Evelyn called it something else. Self-preservation. Evelyn stood in nothing but her plain, functional white underwear while she struggled into her back brace. The thing was harder to fasten than a bridle and harness. She prayed that for today it would be enough. By the end of the day, her back would hurt. Her hip would hurt. Her knees would hurt. She only hoped that her pride remained intact. When it was all one had, one defended it fiercely.

"Evie, hurry up. We're going to be late." Anne Bennett hollered up the stairs. Evelyn would have laughed at the unladylike display, but she was too upset. She was also too tired to remember to correct Anne for calling her Evie. It had been a childhood nickname, and she'd never broken her grandfather of it. The woman he'd married seven years earlier had picked it up as a result. Since the rest of the family used it as well, Anne wasn't letting it go without a fight.

"I'm coming. I can't imagine what your rush is." Neither of them wanted to go to the lawyer's office today. Of course, neither of them had wanted to go to the hospital the month before when Howard Bennett slipped quietly into death, either.

Tears stung Evelyn's eyes, and she pushed them ruthlessly away. She refused to cry, and crying publicly would be the ultimate humiliation. Her grandfather hadn't been the type of man who was comfortable with tears. If he thought his granddaughter and his wife were weeping uncontrollably over his death, it would have made him cringe.

"What are you doing?" Anne watched in disbelief as Evelyn fought with the brace. "You hardly ever wear that thing anymore, though heaven knows we keep trying to get you to. Take it off, get your dress on, grab your cane, and let's go."

"I am not bringing the cane." Evelyn's tone was final, but it never got through to Anne. She took her role as a grandmother quite seriously. Never mind that she wasn't old enough to be her grandmother. Anne was old enough to be her mother, perhaps, but not her grandmother. Evelyn was twenty-five, and Anne was forty-four.

"I am not using the cane," she reiterated as she saw Anne's temper start to build. Evelyn managed to completely fasten the stupid contraption and went for her dress. She looked bigger than she was in the baggy dress, but it hid the brace and was comfortable. All of Evelyn's clothes were comfortable and easy to put on, and in soothing colors much like her bedroom. The clothes had functional lines and were easily managed.

She turned her head side to side, then grabbed a couple of hairpins. She pulled her hair back into a strict bun. Wouldn't the wavy reddish-brown hair that now hung to the middle of her back surprise Sebastian? He'd called her short hair boyish and unfeminine. It was probably the most flattering thing he'd said to her that day, no matter that it was an insult. He'd insulted her in much more hurtful ways than calling her unfeminine.

"Everyone knows you use a cane, Evie." She gave the younger woman an exasperated look when it became apparent that Evelyn wasn't going to listen. "Your cousin David and your cousin Leslie have never made fun of it. They care about you too much to feel anything but sympathy for what you've been through. I've seen it, your sister has seen it, and her husband has seen it when he's at work with you and when you visit. Even the lawyer has seen it. Stop being so sensitive. You had an accident, and you need it."

Evelyn felt the unreasonable panic rise. It always did when she thought about the crippling "accident." She couldn't tell her family she was sure it wasn't an accident. They'd think she was crazy. She thought she was crazy. She had no real memory of what happened. She had been horseback riding alone. Though the trail was a public one, she had been fairly isolated that day. In her more rational moments, she knew it had to have been an accident. Her dreams were her only proof, and she kept them to herself. The ominous dreams threatened her peace of mind, and she refused to discuss them. It would just be another excuse her family would use to try to get her back into therapy.

She took a deep breath and practiced the techniques the therapist had taught her to help her stop the panic attacks. Her heart rate slowed, and the blind panic faded. She knew Anne was watching her and feeling helpless. It was a response she was used to. She hated the sympathy almost as much as she hated the constant supervision.

Evelyn got a better grip on her emotions and concentrated on finishing getting ready. She dabbed a bit of powder on her face and wondered if she should add a bit more makeup. She hadn't seen Sebastian in five years, not since he'd witnessed her most public humiliation. Today Sebastian was the person she didn't want to face. He hadn't seen the cane, and she didn't want him to. She needed to project all the strength she could, although she was sure he knew about the accident. Funny how pride worked. But he'd been there to see almost every humiliating moment of her life, and she'd had enough of looking like a fool.

Sebastian had been there during her awkward teenage years when she'd been having a hard time dealing with her thin, bony body and lack of development. He'd been there when her mother had embarrassed the entire family before running her car off a cliff road because she'd been high and drunk. He'd been her boss and had watched as she'd struggled to do her job while she failed time and again. He'd been there when she'd made a fool of herself by accusing her sister's soon-to-be husband, Sebastian's nephew John, of cheating with her cousin Leslie. Leslie had been dating Sebastian at the time, and he hadn't appreciated the accusation one bit. And he'd been there when she'd been left standing at the altar, her wedding gown swamping her thin body, her limbs visibly trembling. He'd capped it when he quit his job with her grandfather's company earlier that same day, saying he wouldn't take orders from her. Her grandfather was putting her in charge of the company, and

Sebastian predicted that she and her cousin David would ruin the business in less than five years. The final humiliation was that he'd been right. He'd find that out today.

Evelyn did a final check in the mirror. Anne had been seeing to it that Evelyn ate right. Her body had filled in a bit, and she looked pretty good, if you covered up the scars. Her breasts had finally made a late appearance. They might only fill out a B cup, but on her thin, short frame, they looked much bigger. Her hair had lost a lot of the brassy red color and was a more attractive shade of brown with red highlights. Her eyes were still an odd gray color, but with the right makeup and contacts instead of her old glasses, they stood out nicely on her rather plain face. With her small nose, square chin, and high forehead, she wasn't a great beauty, and she knew it. She tried to make up for it with a strong attitude and willpower.

"I'm ready." It was a big fat lie, but Evelyn grabbed her purse anyway. The drive was going to be long, and already she could feel her muscles tensing. The doctor had warned her time and again to lessen her stress levels. If her body relaxed, her muscles wouldn't tighten, and her back and leg wouldn't hurt so much. It was easier said than done.

The minivan Anne had bought five years ago allowed her to stretch out, and she had been so grateful for the legroom that she hadn't reprimanded Anne for buying something that had been solely for her benefit. Evelyn could drive herself now, but in the early days after her accident, driving had hurt more than it was worth. Five years ago, Evelyn had an impractical but cute sports car. With her busted left hip, she just couldn't get herself in and out of the low-slung car. She'd sold it, along with her most prized possession, four years earlier.

Anne helped Evelyn into the van. She drove slower than usual when Evelyn was in the van and tried not to make any sharp turns. Evelyn had assured her time and again that she was much better, but ever since she'd refused to have the last surgery, Anne had been overbearingly protective. At least she was overprotective when she wasn't nagging.

"I'm looking forward to seeing Sebastian. It's been a long time. He called after the funeral. He was sorry he missed it." Anne took another corner and watched Evelyn from the corner of her eye. She didn't know if Sebastian was the sole reason for Evelyn's sudden nerves, but Anne was certain he was at least a small part of the tension that was clear in Evelyn today.

"I wasn't aware that he called." Evelyn wasn't surprised he had, but she hadn't known. He'd kept in touch with Howard and Anne Bennett, but he'd been in Europe the last five years, supposedly learning about the overseas markets. He couldn't have made it any plainer how much he wanted to get away from her.

Evelyn glanced over at Anne. Sebastian had introduced Anne to Howard eight years before, and they'd married a year later. Anne and Sebastian had been friends for a long time. Evelyn knew Anne had been best friends with Sebastian's older sister, and the friendship had been passed along. Anne was closer to Sebastian's age than she was to Howard. Sebastian was thirty-eight this year. His birthday had been last month, Evelyn knew. She knew just about everything about the man. It was funny how you could dislike someone so much and still be fascinated by them.

"He did. I called him, but he was on a business trip and

couldn't fly out for the funeral. When he got back, he offered to come so I wouldn't be alone, but I told him I had you. When he received word from the lawyer that he was mentioned in the will, he called again to say he'd be here."

Evelyn imagined what he had to say about her being the one to console Anne, but she refrained from making any comment. Anne knew that the two of them didn't get along. There was no point in dragging up an old feud.

"Has he visited with John, do you know?" John was not only Evelyn's executive assistant; he was also her sister Kimberly's husband and Sebastian's nephew. John had started with the company shortly before Sebastian had quit. Evelyn had given John a promotion to be her assistant right before her accident, right after Sebastian had left. John thought she did it so she could keep an eye on him. He married her younger sister almost four years ago, just after Evelyn had recovered from the majority of her injuries and had gone back to work. John had been acting as an executive assistant to her grandfather, who had taken back the reins while she recovered from her accident.

On her first day back at work, John told her he was

marrying Kimberly; it was just too bad if she didn't like it, and that she could fire him if she liked. Evelyn had shrugged, ignoring the hurt she'd felt at the verbal attack. But she knew she'd earned it when she'd accused him of having an affair with Leslie. The real question was why he had decided to stay on with her? She knew he was happy with his position in the company and with the large paychecks he received, but that explanation didn't completely satisfy her.

"Sebastian has been out to visit his parents and sister, but I don't think he's seen John. I know they chat from time to time. And of course, Sebastian has been back to see his kids a few times."

Evelyn dropped the subject of Sebastian and closed her eyes for a while. The drive took an hour, and by the time they got there, Evelyn was ready to get out of the van. When she had to sit for long periods, she always took a break and stretched. She managed to get out of the van with the brace on by herself. She could maneuver much more easily with the cane, but she gritted her teeth and headed for the office. Anne trailed slightly behind her, ready to give her a hand should she need it. Evelyn had been trying to exercise her independence, but it was hard when people were always doing things for her without asking if she needed them to.

"Do you need to stop at the bathroom?" Anne held the door open for Evelyn and made it a point to look like it wasn't a calculated move. Anne hated it when Evelyn refused to take her cane. It was a rare occurrence, but this wasn't the first time. Anne had a spare in the back of the van, and she would drag it out if it looked like Evelyn needed it, no matter what Evelyn had to say about it. She understood Evelyn's pride. She also understood her embarrassment. Evelyn had a habit of not letting things go. Her embarrassment over what had happened five years ago was still as prominent today as it had been then. Evelyn put on a good act, but it was only that, an act.

Evelyn shook her head in response to Anne's question. She didn't want to fight with the brace. The sooner they got over with whatever the lawyer had to say, the better. Evelyn knew the company was to be divided equally between Howard's four grandchildren. Evelyn and Kimberly were on one side; David and Leslie were on the other. Neither

Kimberly nor Leslie cared about the chemical company that Howard owned, and each would vote with their respective sibling. The votes always ran two to two. Howard had been the deciding factor in the decision-making at Brown Chemical Labs. David had one idea of how things should run. Evelyn had another. Howard chose between the two. In the last few years, the decisions had swung equally between the two of them. Without Howard, Evelyn knew the company didn't have a chance. She and David would never agree on how to run the company. Howard liked to say that the competition made both of them work harder. Now it would destroy the company Howard had bought out years ago and rebuilt.

Evelyn carefully measured her steps and kept her body rigidly straight. Anne's lips pursed, but she didn't say anything. As the secretary led them into the conference room that was being used for the will reading, Evelyn wasn't worried about upsetting Anne. She was concentrating on the upcoming confrontation. Howard's long-standing attorney, Bruce Bickerstaff, gestured for them to enter the room.

"Come in and have a seat." He took Evelyn's arm and seated her.

Evelyn gave him a slight smile in thanks while internally gritting her teeth. "Thank you, Mr. Bickerstaff."

"No problem." He held a chair for Anne.

Evelyn knew Sebastian was in the room. She refused to look his way, although she could feel he was watching her. He was sitting next to David, who had Leslie, John, and Kimberly between him and her. Evelyn turned her attention to Kimberly. Kimberly was bottle-feeding six-month-old Patrick. John was on the other side talking quietly to Leslie. John was the peacekeeper in the family.

"How is he doing?" Evelyn turned carefully in her seat. Kimberly was frowning at her, and she knew the reason why. Kimberly nagged her just as much as Anne. They thought that between the two of them, they could bully her into having another surgery to fix her back and hip. Evelyn wanted nothing to do with another surgery.

"He's fine. I see you're feeling spry today. Where's your cane, Evie?"

Evelyn was going to correct her sister but dropped it.

Every member of the family called her Evie, even though it annoyed her. Because she was annoyed, she forgot to watch her temper. "I threw it in the trash."

"You didn't!" Kimberly ignored all the turned heads their way.

"Of course, I didn't," she whispered. "Would you please be quiet; you're embarrassing yourself." Evelyn prayed that they weren't overheard.

"I'm not in the least embarrassed. You should be, though. Your behavior lately has been getting out of hand. Perhaps your therapist would have something to say about your outrageous behavior."

Evelyn wanted to tell her that she hadn't been to her therapist lately just to see how she'd react, but John interrupted. He turned and patted Kimberly's shoulder. "Your sister is a big girl. She knows what she's doing. Don't you, Evelyn?"

When Evelyn shifted her eyes, they clashed with Sebastian's instead of John's. That cool reserve was still there, she noted. His piercing green eyes were glued to hers. His hair was still that almost black shade. The light spattering of silver in his hair had barely grown in the last five years. He was still tall and lean. His body was still wrapped in the trappings of sophistication, and they still only barely masked his true personality. He could be cruel when he felt like it. He could be openly passionate when he cared about something. She knew few dared cross him. He'd grown up in rough neighborhoods, and that fact was a permanent part of him. He might look like a businessman, but his rough background was always only partially hidden.

He swamped her five foot four by seven inches. He wasn't the tallest man in the room, but he was the hardest, both in looks and personality. To her, he was a massive presence. It had always been that way. The thirteen years he had on her didn't help alter the impression of power. His age only increased it.

"Hello, Evelyn." Sebastian watched as she shrank into herself.

"Sebastian." Evelyn pulled her eyes from his. That dark, deep, gritty voice made her quiver. It had been too long since she'd seen him last. It had taken years to get used to her reactions to his powerful presence.

"If we're all ready, I'll begin." Bruce interrupted. Evelyn knew he was feeling the increased tension in the room.

Anne took over. As the oldest in the room and Howard's widow, she held the authority. "Please begin." She didn't bother to glance around to see how they all took the decree. Howard had been the driving force behind the family. As his wife, she had wielded the same power.

For the first few minutes, it was Howard's personal effects that were divided up. Anne would keep the house. Everyone expected it. Howard had openly adored his much younger bride. Anne, in turn, loved Howard. The years that separated them had meant nothing. Howard's money meant nothing to Anne. No one doubted either one of their motives for the hasty marriage.

By the time the business was brought up, everyone was satisfied. Nothing in the will had been a surprise. All the various members of the family, except for Evelyn, had their own homes, and they all had their own money. The business was what everyone had come to hear about. So far, Sebastian hadn't been mentioned, and it made Evelyn nervous.

If Howard hadn't left any of his personal effects to Sebastian, then that meant he'd left something of his business. Evelyn felt ill as trepidation gripped her. She didn't want to hear what came next but knew she had to sit through it.

The room was silent as they all waited for what came next.

Want more? Get your copy of This Time Love *today.*

The Hearts Way Series

All Of Me Series

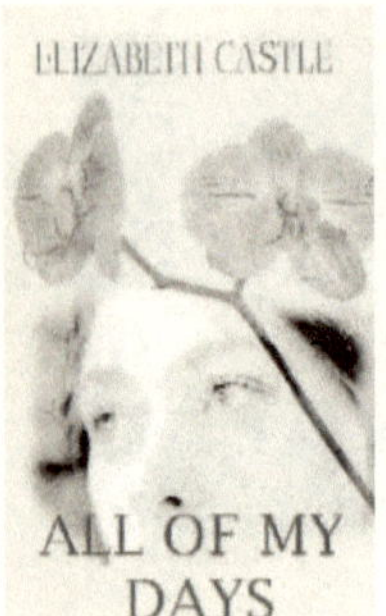

Cantwell Quartet Series

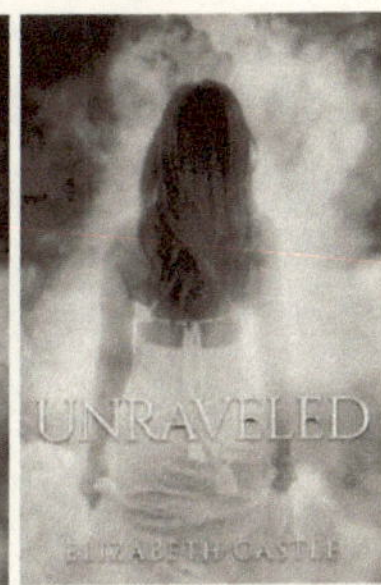

Single Titles & Novellas

Bennett Family Series:

Contemporary "Retro" Romance

www.ingramcontent.com/pod-product-compliance
Lightning Source LLC
Chambersburg PA
CBHW020652010826
48969CB00012B/815